There are houses on the ridge across the valley. There is a big scar, where rock has been quarried out of the escarpment.

All the storm water runs down into the creek.

S
E   W
N

PARK STATION

Maps are usually made with North at the top. But we walked from East to West, so we draw our compass upside-down.

There used to be lots of Cabbage Tree Palms in this valley, but they don't grow here any more.

WOLLI CREEK

Privet grows beside the creek. It can give you hay fever.

The Eora children played in this valley for thousands of years. We learn some of their language.

The water runs from West to East.

The sun is high in the sky when we stop for lunch. Afterwards we play handball and make our Journey Maps.

Little creek

The trees here are tall.

Stone steps

We stop here for recess. It's good to sit down.

We do rubbings of the ripples in the stone.

We stop and talk about how the Eora lived in this valley. They respected the land.

Eucalypts and angophora

Prickly pear

Bird's nest

Pool

Figtree

Ferny gully

GIRRAHWEEN PARK

Coral fern and king fern cling to the rock above the pool. The water is green with algae.

Sandstone escarpment

We sit beneath a rock overhang and draw pictures of the valley. In wet weather the Eora sheltered in caves like this one. We can even see fire marks on the ceiling.

Little cave

Our parents come to pick us up in the afternoon. We've had SO MUCH FUN!

This paperback edition first published in 2013

First published in 2007

Copyright © text Nadia Wheatley 2007
Copyright © illustrations Ken Searle 2007

Allen & Unwin
83 Alexander St
Crows Nest NSW 2065, Australia
Phone: (61 2) 8425 0100
Fax: (61 2) 9906 2218
Email: info@allenandunwin.com
Web: www.allenandunwin.com

FSC
MIX
Paper from
responsible sources
FSC® C124385

A Cataloguing-in-Publication record is available from the National Library of Australia www.trove.nla.org

ISBN 978 1 74331 679 5

Cover design by Ken Searle and Lisa White
Text design by Ken Searle and Lisa White
Typeset by Lisa White

This book was printed in January 2022
at Everbest Printing Co Ltd in 334
Huanshi Road South, Nansha, Guangdong, China

10 9 8 7 6 5 4 3

Teachers notes available from www.allenandunwin.com

GOING BUSH

Nadia Wheatley and Ken Searle

in association with

Al Zahra College, Arncliffe   Rissalah College, Lakemba
Arncliffe Public School   Arncliffe West Infants Public School
Athelstane Public School   Bexley Public School
Our Lady of Fatima, Kingsgrove   St Francis Xavier's, Arncliffe

ALLEN&UNWIN
SYDNEY · MELBOURNE · AUCKLAND · LONDON

KEY

1 Afia and Omar's school:
   Rissalah College, Lakemba

2 Christine and Liam's school:
   Our Lady of Fatima, Kingsgrove

3 Hannah and Nathan's school:
   Bexley Public School

4 Chaltu and Alban's school:
   Athelstane Public School

5 Dora and Sarah's school:
   St Francis Xavier's, Arncliffe

6 Alannah and Daniel's school:
   Arncliffe West Infants Public School

7 Lily and Phillip's school:
   Arncliffe Public School

8 Fatima and Mohammed's school:
   Al Zahra College, Arncliffe

------- The bush walk

Harmony
is happiness,
peace and joy,
friendship,
and faith in each other.
Phillip

COOKS RIVER

Old Canterbury Road

Friendship
is when
you have company.
Alannah

WOLLI CREEK

Kingsgrove Rd

King Georges Road

Stoney Creek Rd

Forest Rd

Princes Highway

Syd
Air

BOTANY
BAY

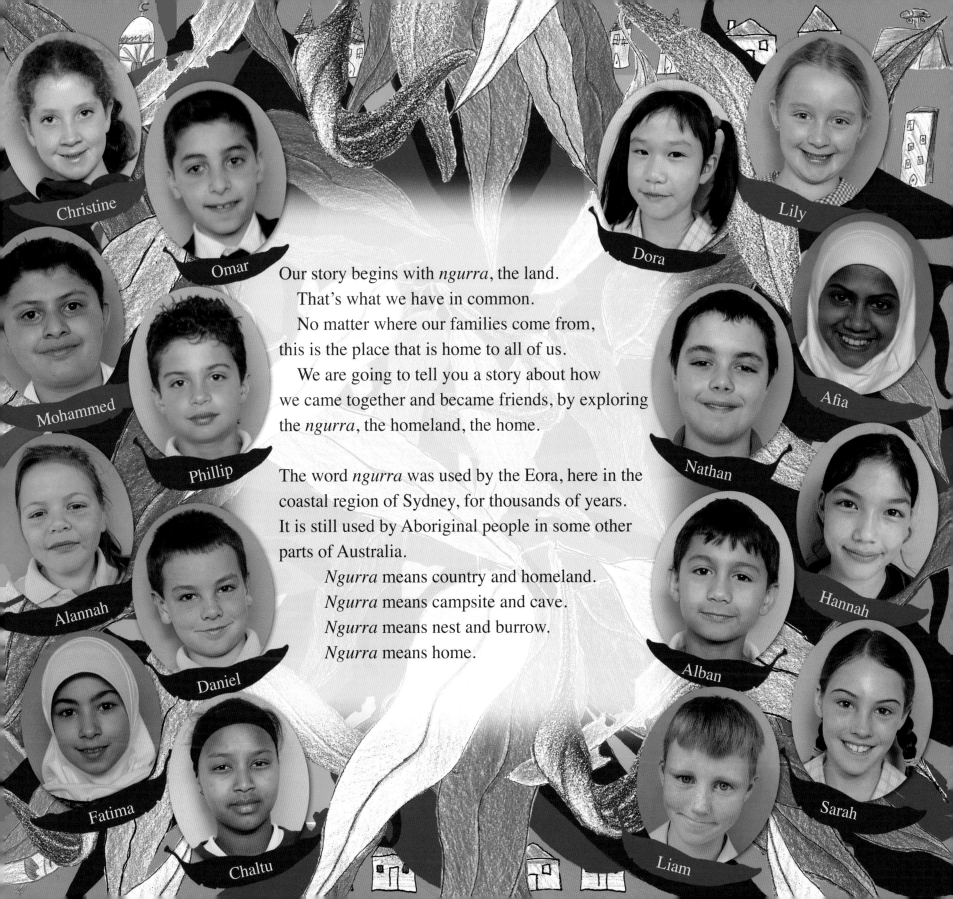

Christine

Omar

Dora

Lily

Mohammed

Afia

Phillip

Nathan

Alannah

Hannah

Daniel

Alban

Fatima

Liam

Chaltu

Sarah

Our story begins with *ngurra*, the land.

That's what we have in common.

No matter where our families come from, this is the place that is home to all of us.

We are going to tell you a story about how we came together and became friends, by exploring the *ngurra*, the homeland, the home.

The word *ngurra* was used by the Eora, here in the coastal region of Sydney, for thousands of years. It is still used by Aboriginal people in some other parts of Australia.

Ngurra means country and homeland.

Ngurra means campsite and cave.

Ngurra means nest and burrow.

Ngurra means home.

It is spring when we make our journey. This is the season when the bush bursts into new growth. For us, this is a time for the growth of new friendships.

I'm feeling quite shy to meet new kids
and I hope I've got everything I need.
Hannah

I haven't been here before
and I don't know what to expect.
Mohammed

I am very excited because
this is my first bushwalk.
Dora

Like an egg opening
a tree overblossoming
a waterfall full of action —
That's the seeds growing
new life.
Hannah

The Wolli Creek Valley has been a *muru* (pathway) for thousands of years. The name 'Wolli' is Aboriginal. It may mean 'camping place'. Certainly, the Eora (people) lived in this valley and looked after it. They used the creek flats and the ridges as a track to the south-west.

These days, people travel the valley in different ways. We can hear trains on the railway line. In a tunnel nearby, cars and trucks are thundering along the expressway. Above us, planes are taking off and landing. But we still feel the harmony of the bush all around us.

**PAYING RESPECT TO COUNTRY
AND THE CUSTODIANS**

We acknowledge
the traditional owners of the land
on which we live and learn.
We pay our respects to them
for their care of the land
over countless generations.
We hope they will walk with us
on our journey,
as we share friendship together.

As we set off, we start to learn about the plants that grow in the bush. To us, they just seem like flowers and trees, but to the traditional owners, the bush was like a big supermarket.

Look! There's a clump of mistletoe growing high up in that tree. For the Eora, the berries of this plant were good food, and the bark was used as a medicine for coughs and colds.

Seeds of wattle and lomandra were ground up to make flour. This was mixed with water, and the flat bread was cooked on the ashes of the fire. The leaf base of the lomandra was nibbled as a snack, and wattle gum soaked in honey was eaten as a lolly.

In the past there were lots of *daranggara* (cabbage trees) growing in the Wolli Creek Valley. The Eora ate the buds of these trees, and plaited the leaves to make baskets and bags.

When the first settlers came here, they called the creek Cabbage Tree Creek. They made hats out of the fronds. So many of the palms were used that, slowly slowly, they became extinct. The last *daranggara* grew in the valley in the 1920s.

Afia

Near the bank of the creek there is a stand of *gurrundurrung*. The bark of these trees feels like paper, and it peels off in sheets.

The Eora used thick layers of this paperbark to make their *ngurra* (shelters). In wet weather, the bark was worn like a cloak. A small piece of bark twisted at each end made a food container, and the children used to tie a lump of bark with vine-string to make a ball.

Gurrundurrung —
Leaves whisper and rustle,
sharp as dragon tongues.
The rusty soft bark
dry and sour,
like paper.

Hannah

On the bushwalk we have clipboards and paper for drawing and writing. Some kids bring little plastic boxes for collecting soil and stones and sticks and fallen leaves and bits of burnt wood. We each have a camera, and we often stop to take photos.

Alban

Our next stop is the creek.

In the past, the salt water coming up from Botany Bay met the fresh water that runs down the ridges of the valley. Now the weir makes a barrier, except when there's heavy rain.

The trees beside the creek tell us history. On the saltwater side, casuarinas grow. Their leaves are thin, like needles, and they make a thick carpet when they fall to the ground.

On the eastern side is the salty water. You can tell because it looks cleaner. The tide comes in and out, twice a day, bringing the water from the ocean.

Daniel

Beside the creek —
Casuarinas
standing high,
brown and mighty.
Big roots grip the ground,
searching deep for water
in this horrible drought.

Liam

On the freshwater banks, willow trees remind us of the homesick English settlers, who brought the plants to make the strange country look like home. Now willows are a pest. They clog the waterways.

The red-flowered coral is another tree that isn't native to Australia.

The water on the western side of the weir is dirty, and there are bubbles of scum. Sticks and paper are trapped there. I see algae and moss growing.

Alannah

Ducks bobbing,
darting at their prey —
flashes of moving colour.

Dora

Mallards cruise the creek,
their emerald chests ablaze.
The egret stalks the shallows,
searching for fish.

Nathan

Although the city is all around us, it isn't hard for us to imagine how people lived in this *ngurra* in the past.

In traditional times, families were small. When the weather was dry, the Eora camped beside the fresh water in paperbark shelters. Their *nuwi* (canoes) were made from the casuarina trees.

It took a quarter of an hour to walk from here to the place where the creek joins the river, and then it was a short journey to Gamay (Botany Bay). Here in the creek the mullet and flathead were easy to catch. A little further east, in the saltwater estuary, were crabs and oysters and mussels.

All the coastal children could swim, almost as soon as they could walk. In the Wolli Creek there were a number of good *bugi*-holes.

For fishing, the Eora men used a harpoon with sharp prongs. They dived from the rocks into the water, and speared the fish.

The women went out fishing in canoes. They used hooks made of shell, attached to lines which they made from vines. They often burned a little fire in the canoe, so they could cook the fish and eat it, if they got a bit hungry. Groups of women and children used to bring fish and crabs and shellfish back to their freshwater campsites.

Hannah

Aboriginal families still live in this *ngurra*, and they still get food in traditional ways. Daniel tells us a story about getting bush tucker.

We sometimes catch yabbies — I really love yabbies! They live in the banks of creeks or rivers.

I catch yabbies by putting a little piece of meat on a string. Then I tie fish guts on. I throw the line in the water and then I sit there and wait till I feel something come on the end of the line. Then I quickly pull the yabby out and catch it, or sometimes I use a net. When the basket is full, I put the yabbies in a billy boil with hot water and cook them. Then I eat them!

me

cousin in water

Fish guts →

yaby basket

yaby and bait

After visiting the weir, we set off down the *muru* (path) that skirts around the bottom of Nannygoat Hill.

This is easy walking, on a track that follows the natural lie of the land. It feels as if feet have been travelling along here for thousands of years.

Sometimes when we look down from the path we can see the creek, snaking along below us.

Over the edge of the ridge we spot a grass tree. It is amazing to see one, so close to the city.

Grass trees grow very slowly. This one could be hundreds of years old. It was probably here when the Eora used to walk along the track.

Aborigines used the stem of the grass tree to make spear shafts and they used the resin as a glue, to attach barbs of shell or bone. They also ate the bud of the tree, and they made cordial from the sweet flowers.

Small to medium-size trees and bushes grow here, such as wattles and banksias, tea-tree and kunzea. The banksia cones look like funny faces.

Vines tangling through the bush have little flowers — red and pinky-white and purple. The Eora used the strong stems of these plants to make fishing line and string. The children sometimes used to play games with string, and they used vines as skipping ropes.

On the open ridge, there's a lot of bracken fern. The root was eaten as a vegetable, just like we eat carrots.

The rocks in the valley are sandstone. If this stone breaks down and becomes soil, it is very sandy. There aren't many nutrients in it, and water runs through it quickly. The plants growing in this *ngurra* (habitat) are adapted to these hard conditions.

Christine

The sun is starting to climb in the sky when we stop at the logs for a rest. This is a shady place, where the bushes make an archway across the path.

We shut our eyes for two whole minutes and sit in silence, listening to the noises around us.

Helicopters throbbing...
Trains rattling...
Lizards rustling...
Planes zooming...
Birds calling...
Trees sighing...
Traffic thrumming...
Leaves swishing...
Twigs snapping...
Machines clanking...

Then we make an orchestra of the sounds.

It's hard to tell the difference between the real noises and us!

Trees
Waving through the wind —
twigs falling,
insects rumbling,
green leaves spinning,
flowers closing.
Chaltu

The *muru* takes us down towards the creek. If we stand on the high bank, we can see into the wetland, where willow trees and bulrushes grow.

Algae, green as grass.
Reeds, soft as feathers.
Leaves, floating on the water.
Chaltu

Around a bend, we find ourselves in a tiny patch of rainforest. The tree canopy is so dense that we can't see the sky, but we can still hear birds.

Here the soil is dark and moist, and the bush smells different, too. This is a place of ferns and shadows. The rocks are green with moss and lichen.

Many of the plants in this rainforest are called 'exotic'. This means that they belong to other countries. Privet, lantana and morning glory have taken over this part of the valley.

Most of the plants here are weeds. The seeds are often brought by birds or the wind, but sometimes people dump their garden rubbish at the edge of the bush, and it spreads. Another problem is caused when fertiliser runs off into the valley. This makes the soil too rich for native plants, and encourages weeds to grow.

Hannah

The Eora looked after the land,
cared for the land,
respected the land
and the seasons.

They cared for the animals
and the trees.

They looked after each other
and everything around them.
Sacred.

Lily

We climb up some steep stone steps that bring us to the bottom of the escarpment.

Underneath the rock overhang there is a small concrete pool which was built in the 1920s as a swimming hole. This is where we stop for recess.

While we are eating, we talk about how other people have picnicked in this place, in the past.

In the bush nearby we see a nest. Birds like to come here to have a drink — just as we're doing.

LUNCH

I feel happy when I am with a friend.
I feel peace when we play together.
We share and have lots of joy.

When I am with a friend
I don't have to do anything by myself.

Afia

On top of the cliff there are houses. In the bush below we see a prickly pear that has escaped from one of the gardens. In southern Europe people love to eat the fleshy pink fruit, but in Australia this plant is a pest. When we touch it, we get spikes in our fingers.

At one time Russell's Pool would have been full, but now the water is only a few centimetres deep. In it there is waterweed and algae, and sometimes frogspawn. Coral fern and king fern cling to the rock overhang above the pool.

The shallow water of the pool is a breeding ground for frogs. This could have something to do with the king fern, which is a frog-attracting plant.

The Brown Striped Marsh Frog lives here. It is brown to light grey, with a series of dark, irregular stripes across its body.

Nathan

As we journey on around the escarpment, the path becomes very narrow. It is like walking on a shelf. To our right, the rock towers above us. To our left, the ridge drops down to the creek. The soil here is dry and sandy.

On the surface of the stone, moss and lichen grow. From pockets of soil in the crevices, king ferns sprout.

When we do crayon rubbings of the sandstone, the ripples beneath our fingers tell a story...

Once upon a time, Australia and Antarctica were joined together as one continent, called Gondwanaland.

About two hundred and thirty million years ago, a big sand river flowed from Antarctica, all the way to this area. At the river mouth, tonnes of sand were dumped. When the wet sand hardened, it formed the sandstone that lies under the Sydney Basin.

Six thousand years ago, the level of the sea rose and flooded some of the land. This made Botany Bay, the Cooks River and Wolli Creek.

It is amazing how you can still see the flow of the massive river in the ripples of the sandstone.

Liam and Christine

Stone cliffs make me feel
like I am going to fall off —
the stone
is so big!
Alannah

Sandstone escarpments
worn and weathered with wind —
rough, strong and protective.
Dora

In the shade of a rock overhang, we all sit and do a drawing. From this high point we can look right out over the valley. Drawing is a really good way to understand the shape of the *ngurra*. If you take a photo you only look for a second, but if you do a drawing you have to concentrate on the shapes of the land for a much longer time.

While we are working, we pick up the smells and sounds of the bush. We start to feel comfortable with the land, and with each other.

When the first Europeans came to this area, there were so many trees that it was described as a forest. Most of the trees were cut down, but this north side of the valley was too steep for anyone to clear.

When you look across to the ridge on the other side, you can see the scars of quarries in the rock. Sandstone was cut out in blocks, to build houses.

Omar and Sarah

The sandstone of this valley has made habitats for plants and animals and people for thousands of years.

In the sand under the overhang, we see tracks of insects and lizards. Fire marks on the ceiling of the cave show that people have camped here.

Beside the cave, the roots of a fig tree dig into a crevice. It's hard to believe that such a big tree can get enough nourishment from such a tiny amount of soil and water.

Stone —
Rough, rippling, smooth.
Aboriginal people used it for shelter.
Bull ants and spiders, too.

Sarah

When the escarpment ends, the track leads down into a small sheltered gully. This is the sort of *ngurra* where the Eora camped in wet weather. There is a little cave set into the hill, and a tiny watercourse runs down to the creek.

We map how life might have been for the families who lived here.

The women and children caught small animals, such as possums and birds and lizards, and they collected insects and grubs. They gathered fruit and vegetables, and seeds for making bread. They made baskets and coolamons to carry the food back to camp.

The men travelled out of the valley to hunt for big animals such as kangaroos and emus. They used spears made from the pointy spike of the grass tree, and special throwing sticks called woomeras.

Omar and Phillip

Eora —
People caring
for everything in the land.
Only taking what is needed.
Respect.
Liam

The Eora loved the land very much and they
cared for the beautiful Wolli Creek valley.
They regularly burned the undergrowth,
to clean up the bush. After the fires the seeds
would pop open and the plants would
grow, and so the animals would come
into the valley.
Sarah

Fire for burning,
Fire for hunting,
Fire for cooking,
Fire for the opening of the seeds.
Red, yellow, orange —
These are the colours of fire.
Mohammed

Bark —
Hard and brown
Smooth or rough
Edgy, cracked —
Good for making medicines.
Omar

As the path takes us on, we find ourselves once again in a new sort of *ngurra*.

Here the soil is a little bit different, because the sandstone has clay on top of it. Clay holds more moisture than sand, and so a forest of tall trees is able to grow. There is bracken and lomandra, but the understorey of the bush is a lot more open than it was at the beginning of our walk.

We see where a fire went through last summer and blackened the trees.

We touch the trunks of three different types of tree.

The bark of the red bloodwood is thick and chunky, and the bright sap is sticky beneath our fingers.

The bark of the peppermint gum is coarse and rough, like strands of old rope.

The trunk of the smooth-barked apple is pink and purple. It feels like satin.

Tree —
Leaves swaying in the wind,
Roots gripping in the ground.
Bark rough and jagged.
Dora

Trees —
Grassy smells
Hard, rough bark
Juicy, fleshy, yummy fruit
Gooey sap, rippling down like a tap.
Fatima

By now the sun is high in the sky, and everybody is very hungry. There is just one last glimpse of the creek before we make our way up the hill to the picnic area. Food tastes different in the bush.

When lunch is finished, we play handball. It's funny to think that just last week we were all strangers, but now we are eating and playing together as a group.

All Aboriginal kids played games. These were for fun, but they were also a way to learn survival skills. Group games included memory games and tracking games. Adults often joined in, to help their children learn.

The Eora children also enjoyed playing in the water and climbing trees. They played with balls and spinning tops and dolls, and they often liked to make *ngurra ngurra* (cubby houses).

Other children have played in this valley for thousands and thousands of years. We have been walking in their footsteps all day.

Liam and Sarah

To eat, to drink, to play, to live together
is friendship.
To feel love, joy, happiness, and faith together
is friendship.
To feel welcome and harmony
is friendship.
To feel a sense of belonging
is friendship.
Eora — the People
Together, as one.

Lily

After the game is over, we put some big pieces of paper on the tables and make journey maps.

We talk about where we have been today, and what we have seen. We all remember different things, or we remember the same things a little bit differently.

If we put all our memories together, we end up with one big story.

Our walk through the bush has ended, but a whole new adventure is just beginning.
It's time to start making our story into a book...

On this journey I experienced the bush and I experienced life.
I also found a brand-new way to learn, and know new things.

Christine

Our story begins with *ngurra*, the land.
That's what we have in common.
No matter where our families come
from, this is the place that we call home.

PLANT GLOSSARY

This plant glossary only lists the plants named in *Going Bush*.
Hundreds of plants are indigenous to this area. Sometimes more
than one variety of a plant species is to be found in the valley.

Scientific name	Common name
Indigenous plants	
Acacia longifolia	Sydney Golden Wattle
Acacia suaveolens	Sweet-scented Wattle
Acacia terminalis	Sunshine Wattle
Acacia ulicifolia	Prickly Moses
Allocasuarina littoralis	Casuarina
Amyemer congener	Mistletoe
Angophora costata	Smooth-barked Apple
Banksia serrata	Old Man Banksia
Banksia integrifolia	Coastal Banksia
Calochlaena dubia	Soft (or False) Bracken Fern
Eucalyptus gummifera	Red Bloodwood
Eucalyptus piperita	Sydney Peppermint
Ficus rubiginosa	Port Jackson Fig
Gleichenia dicarpa	Coral Fern
Kunzea ambigua	Tick Bush
Leptospermum polygalifolium	Tea-tree
Lomandra longifolia	Mat-rush
Melaleuca styphelioides	Paperbark
Pteridium esculentum	Bracken Fern
Todea barbara	King Fern
Xanthorrhoea australis	Grass Tree
Exotic plants	
Erythrina sykesii	Coral Tree
Ipomoea indica	Morning Glory
Lantana camara	Lantana
Ligustrum lucidum	Large-leaved Privet
Ligustrum sinense	Small-leaved Privet
Opuntia stricta	Prickly Pear
Salix babylonica	Weeping Willow

ABORIGINAL GLOSSARY

This glossary only lists words found in *Going Bush*.
It has been compiled from early settler word-lists, checked with
Jakelin Troy, *The Sydney Language*, 1993. There are many
variations in the spelling of Aboriginal languages.

bugi	swim
daranggara	Cabbage Tree Palm
Eora	people; collective name for the clans of the coastal region around Port Jackson and Botany Bay
gumun	Casuarina
gurrundurrung.	Paperbark Tree
muru	path
ngurra	country, traditional land, homeland, environment, habitat, nest, burrow, campsite, cave, home
nuwi	canoe(s)

ACKNOWLEDGEMENTS

Our thanks go first to Rose-Marie Hoekstra, Principal of Our Lady of Fatima School Kingsgrove in 2005, who invited us to work with the Inter-school Harmony Committee and who gave us freedom to interpret and develop the theme of Harmony. This project could not have happened without Rose-Marie's commitment and particular vision.

We are also indebted to Ahmad Mokachar, Principal of Al Zahra College, who provided our group with a room and resources. Everyone at Al Zahra College made us all feel welcome, especially Rania Ibrahim and Anaya Matar in the office.

We are very grateful to Anne Morgan, teacher-librarian from Our Lady of Fatima, who was our main support teacher, and who provided continuity for the students and their parents.

Two parents, Francine Commeignes and Kathleen Morgan, worked with us and the children in the classroom.

We would also like to thank the principals from the Inter-school Harmony Committee who supported the project, and the staff members from the other schools who acted as support teachers.

During the eight weeks that we worked with the students, the project was financed primarily through moneys raised during a dinner held by Al Zahra College commemorating International Peace Day and the birth of Imam Mahdi. The Catholic Education Office Sydney also provided financial support.

Our preparation for the bushwalk was done under the guidance of Peter Stevens and Judy Finlason, from the Wolli Creek Preservation Society. Debra Little helped with the glossary.

The educational principles underlying our work with the students reflect the Papunya Model of Education, which was developed by Anangu staff and Diane de Vere at Papunya School (Northern Territory) during the 1990s. This model puts country (*ngurra*) at the core of the curriculum, and values the knowledge which students bring from their homes and communities. The Learning Journeys and Circle Stories which we created with the students were first developed at Papunya.

While so many people played a significant role in this project, our deepest gratitude goes to the families of the sixteen students who took part. We thank them for their trust in us.

Finally, we would like to congratulate the children themselves — for their brilliant writing and art, for their hard work and good humour, and for the harmony that they have created.

Nadia Wheatley and Ken Searle

HOW TO GO BUSH

Whoever you are, and wherever your home is, you too can go bush!

The bushland valley that we explored for this book was close to the centre of a city, with a highway and a railway line nearby, and an aeroplane flight path overhead.

No matter where you live, you are sure to find a little patch of wild land, or you can walk around your suburb and get to know the trees growing on the nature strips and in the parks.

Going bush is a way of looking and thinking and feeling and exploring. It's about who you are, not where you are.

As you make your own bush journeys, these are some of the things you might like to do …

Acknowledging the Traditional Custodians

When you are ready to begin your bush walk, take a moment to sit down quietly as the children are doing on page 5, and pay your respects to the Aboriginal people who for thousands of years have looked after the part of Australia where you live.

Make an Orchestra of Sounds

While you are sitting, shut your eyes and listen to all the different sounds around you, as the children are doing on pages 14–15.

Can you hear birds calling, or the rustle of wind in the trees? Can you hear traffic or machines? Can you hear other people?

Now you've been quiet, it's time to make a noise! See if you can mimic all the different sounds you have heard. First do this for each individual noise. And then, if you are in a group, let everybody choose a noise, and make an orchestra of the sounds.

Make a Poem about a Tree

Sit down near a tree, preferably a native Australian tree, but any tree will do.

Read out loud some tree poems from *Going Bush*. You could try Hannah's poems on pages 4 and 7, Liam's poem on page 8, Chaltu's poem on page 15, or the poems by Dora and Fatima on page 27.

Touch your tree, from the roots up as far up as you can reach. Collect any bark, leaves, twigs, seedpods or flowers that have fallen on the ground. How do all these things fit together to make the tree? What sort of birds or animals might live in the tree? How does your tree make the world a better place?

Make a quick sketch of your tree, to help you understand its shape. Then sketch or trace a leaf. If your tree has flowers or seedpods, draw them as well.

Make a list of the words you might use in a tree poem. For example:
Nouns: trunk, branches, bark, twigs, leaf, leaves, roots, seedpods, flowers, birds, cicadas, breeze, earth, sky
Verbs: grow, stretch, move, dance, rustle, murmur, shake
Adjectives: green, dry, brittle, smooth, hard, rough, dark, papery, aromatic, slender, thick, tall, clumpy
Adverbs: gracefully, gently, quickly, slowly, quietly

Now you are ready to write a short tree-poem like the ones that the children wrote for *Going Bush*. You only need to write a few lines; aim for between three and six.

Don't use rhyme or acrostic (letters down the page). Just make a word-picture to describe the actual tree that you are sitting near.

When you are back home or in the classroom, you might like to copy your tree sketch and your tree poem onto a piece of clean paper. Make borders with rubbings of the bark, or with drawings of leaves, flowers and seedpods.

Now you know how to make a tree-poem, you could use the same method to write about other things you have encountered in your journey, such as water, birds, rocks, sky, friendship …

Make a Coolamon

The children in our story used paperbark and string to make coolamons, which they filled with leaves and gumnuts and shells and other things they collected in the bush. (See the photo below.)

Instead of paperbark, you can use brown craft paper, or any strong paper. Just cut it into a rectangle about 20 cm x 40 cm. If you like, you can decorate your paper on both sides with coloured pencils or marker-pens. You might like to draw leaves and gumnuts and bush flowers.

Then crumple together one end of the paper, and ask a friend to tie a piece of string around it. (You could use a rubber band instead of string.) Then do the same with the other end.

Make a Rubbing of Rock or Bark

You can make a rubbing of rock, as the children are doing on pages 20–21, or you can do a rubbing of tree bark. Just hold a piece of paper against the surface, and scribble over it with a dark-coloured crayon until the paper is covered. You will need to press hard.

If you like, you can cut up the rubbing into strips and use it for the borders of a picture.

Make a New Friend

If you are making your bush journey as a group, walk with someone who isn't already one of your close friends. When you are sitting down to have a rest, read out loud to each other the poems by Afia on page 18 and by Lily on page 29. What are the important qualities you look for in a friend?

Make a Journey Map

Making a journey map at the end of your bush walk is the best way to remember where you have been and what you have done.

It's good to do this activity as a group of half a dozen, but even two or three people are enough. If there are more than eight of you, break into two groups.

Look at the journey map at the front and back of the book, and then have a look at what the children are doing on pages 28–29.

Use a big piece of paper cut from a roll. (A good size is about 1 metre x 2.5 metres). If you don't have a roll of paper, use a large rectangular piece of cardboard, maybe cut from an old box. Lay it out on a picnic table or on the ground. Make yourselves comfortable sitting or standing around it.

Using coloured marker-pens or pencils, put the start of your journey at the left-hand side of the paper and the end of your journey at the right. Draw the line of the pathway of your journey along the centre of the sheet. (Use the journey map in this book as your model.)

Then, working together, draw and write into the map the important things that you remember from your bush walk. These might include particular trees, rocks and other landmarks, or places where you crossed a road. Did you see water? What was the weather doing? What noises did you hear? Where did you stop to rest?

Use a combination of words and pictures, and try to describe your feelings as well as the things you have seen and heard.

As the children say on page 29: 'We all remember different things, or we remember the same things a little bit differently. If we all put our memories together, we end up with one big story.'

Have fun going bush!

Best wishes,

Nadia and *Ken*

Nadia Wheatley is an award-winning author whose books reflect a commitment to issues of Reconciliation, social justice and the conservation of the environment. She has been nominated by IBBY Australia for the 2014 Hans Christian Andersen Award for Writing – the highest international recognition given to a living author whose complete works have made a lasting contribution to children's literature.

Ken Searle is best known for the cityscapes that he has exhibited during a forty-year career as an artist. In his illustration and design he draws upon the same sense of composition to take the reader on a journey through the landscape of the book.

During the period 1998 to 2001, Nadia and Ken worked as consultants at the school at Papunya (an Aboriginal community in the Northern Territory), where they assisted Anangu staff and students to develop resources for the school's Indigenous curriculum. Through this experience, Nadia and Ken were introduced to the Indigenous principles of learning that have inspired and informed the non-fiction books they have produced – whether as author, illustrator, designer, mentor or compiler – and which are showcased on this page.

This way of learning recognises country (or the environment) as both the starting point and the centre of all understanding. It is also a way of learning that is collaborative, holistic and experiential.

In 2005, when Nadia and Ken were invited to develop a Harmony project with sixteen culturally-diverse children from Sydney's south-west, they began with the 'country' of the local area where the children lived. After experiencing the harmony of the natural environment, the children were encouraged to learn about harmony between the traditional owners and the land, and to find harmony in working and playing together.

As one of the students summed up the project: 'On this journey I experienced the bush and I experienced life. I also found a brand new way to learn, and know new things.'

Papunya School Book of Country and History

Papunya School
with Nadia Wheatley and Ken Searle

A collaborative account of the history of this internationally famous Western Desert community, told from the point of view of Papunya Elders and young people. As an example of two-way learning, this outstanding picture book is a profound metaphor for Reconciliation

Winner, NSW Premier's Young People's History Award, 2002
Winner, Award for Excellence in Educational Publishing, 2002
Winner, CBCA Eve Pownall Award, 2002

When I Was Little, Like You

Mary Malbunka

With evocative words and stunning pictures done in both traditional and European style, Pintupi-Luritja artist Mary Malbunka tells her own story of learning about her environment and her culture when she was growing up in the Western Desert community of Papunya during the 1960s.

Shortlisted, NSW Premier's Young People's History Prize, 2004
Shortlisted, NSW Literary Awards, Patricia Wrightson Prize, 2004
Shortlisted, CBCA Eve Pownall Award, 2004

Walking with the Seasons in Kakadu

Diane Lucas
illustrated by Ken Searle

This sumptuous book, which traces the annual cycle of the six Aboriginal seasons of the Top End of our continent, invites us to journey with the traditional owners of Kakadu and to connect with the birds, plants and animals of that unique environment.

Shortlisted, Wilderness Society Environment Award, 2004
Shortlisted, Award for Excellence in Educational Publishing, 2004

Playground: Listening to Stories from Country and from Inside the Heart

compiled by Nadia Wheatley
illustrated by Ken Searle

With historical and contemporary photographs, artwork by leading Indigenous artists, and new colour illustrations throughout, this compilation of Indigenous stories gives a fascinating insight into Aboriginal childhood, both traditional and contemporary.

Winner, Award for Excellence in Educational Publishing, 2012
Shortlisted, NSW Premier's Young People's History Award, 2012
Shortlisted, CBCA Eve Pownall Award, 2012

Going Bush

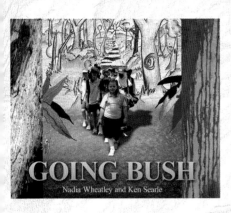

Nadia Wheatley
illustrated by Ken Searle

As children from different cultural backgrounds explore a patch of inner-city bushland, they make discoveries about the land they share and the things they have in common. A model for the way harmony can be shared across Australian society.

Winner, Award for Excellence in Educational Publishing, 2007
Winner, Wilderness Society Children's Literature Award, 2008
Winner, Speech Pathology Book of the Year Award, 2008

Australians All: a History of Growing Up from the Ice Age to the Apology

Nadia Wheatley
illustrated by Ken Searle

Meticulously researched, beautifully written and lavishly illustrated with a combination of facsimile images (photographs, paintings, cartoons etc) and new illustrations, *Australians All* helps us understand who we are, and how we belong to the land we all share. It also shows us who we might be.

Teachers' notes for all these titles are available at www.allenandunwin.com

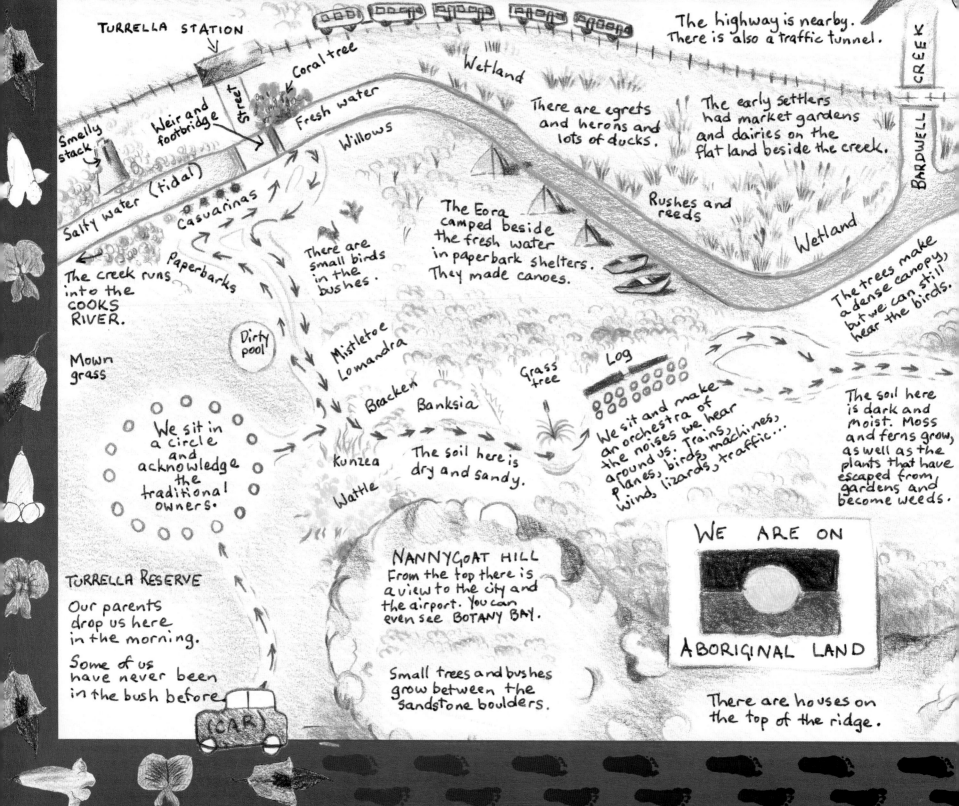

TURRELLA STATION

The highway is nearby. There is also a traffic tunnel.

BARDWELL CREEK

Coral tree

Street

Weir and footbridge

Fresh water

Smelly stack

Salty water (tidal)

Wetland

The creek runs into the COOKS RIVER.

Casuarinas

Willows

Paperbarks

There are egrets and herons and lots of ducks.

The early settlers had market gardens and dairies on the flat land beside the creek.

There are small birds in the bushes.

The Eora camped beside the fresh water in paperbark shelters. They made canoes.

Rushes and reeds

Wetland

The trees make a dense canopy, but we can still hear the birds.

Mown grass

Dirty pool

Mistletoe Lomandra

Bracken

Banksia

Grass tree

Log

Kunzea

The soil here is dry and sandy.

Wattle

We sit in a circle and acknowledge the traditional owners.

We sit and make an orchestra of the noises we hear around us. Trains, planes, birds, machines, winds, lizards, traffic...

The soil here is dark and moist. Moss and ferns grow, as well as the plants that have escaped from gardens and become weeds.

TURRELLA RESERVE

Our parents drop us here in the morning.

Some of us have never been in the bush before.

(CAR)

NANNYGOAT HILL
From the top there is a view to the city and the airport. You can even see BOTANY BAY.

Small trees and bushes grow between the sandstone boulders.

WE ARE ON ABORIGINAL LAND

There are houses on the top of the ridge.